Modjadji

The Rain Queen from South Africa

Written by Pankaj Sulodia
Illustrations by Octavia Spinney

Ringwood Waldorf School Press
www.ringwoodwaldorfschool.org.uk
2022

upon a time, a very long time ago, in the thern part of Africa, there lived a Chief and his fe. They had no children of their own. The Chief uled over the land covering fields and villages. Both the Chief and his wife were kind people and lived a comfortable life. The only wish they had was to have a child. However, no matter how much they wished for or how much they prayed for one, they had neither a daughter nor a son.

4

One day while the Chief was watching his herd while standing on one leg like a big stork bird, he noticed there was something in the bush near him. When he looked carefully he saw that there was a baby goat in there. A baby goat is called a kid.

The kid looked unwell and sleepy. The Chief knew that the kid was dehydrated and would not live if not taken care of. He picked up the kid and gave it some water from his bag. Along with his cows, he brought the kid with him to his house.

The Chief and his wife looked after the kid just like their own child and within a few weeks the kid was full of life, jumping around and making both the Chief and his wife laugh.

One night while the Chief's wife was asleep she had a dream. In her dream she saw a goat which magically turned into a little baby girl. The next morning she told her husband about her dream. The Chief and his wife did not think much of the dream and went on doing their daily work.

Not long after the dream, the Chief's wife gave birth to a baby girl. Both the Chief and his wife were over the moon. They threw a party and invited all the villagers. There was lots of delicious food and dancing and the party went on from dusk to dawn.

Despite the celebration the Chief looked sad that night. When his wife asked him about it, he admitted that he was worried about who would be the next Chief after him. Because only a son was allowed to take the position of the Chief, not a daughter. His wife gave him a hug and reassured him that it would all work out. The Chief and his wife named their daughter Modjadji.

As a child Modjadji was very helpful around the house and always kind and polite. By the time she was 7 years old she had learned how to work on the land and was a great help to her father in the field. Her father taught her how to use a bow and arrow.

On her 8th birthday her father gave her a very special bow made out of African blackwood. It was strung with a leather thong. Modjadji made her own arrows with straight and thin branches from the trees.

Modjadji always carried her bow with her wherever she went. She loved taking her cows to pasture over the hill where the grass was all fresh and green from the African rains. She would watch her herd as she stood on one leg, like a big stork bird.

One day Modjadji was out walking when she found a young eagle that had fallen from its nest. The young bird was struggling and couldn't move properly. Modjadji picked the bird up and took it home and began to care for it. She made a place for the eagle to stay and each day shared some of her food with it. Modjadji named the young eagle Thunder.

Thunder grew up to become a great big eagle. One evening when Modjadji went to feed Thunder she was horrified to see that Thunder wasn't there. Modjadji began to cry but her mother and father hugged her and reassured her that Thunder was likely to be well and healthy and to have gone back to his own habitat. Modjadji understood what her parents were saying but she missed her dear eagle very much and had watery eyes.

Time passed by and Modjadji and her little family lived happily until a great drought struck their beautiful land. There was no rain for many months. People as well as the wild creatures were struggling to survive.

Modjadji went everyday to the top of the hill to speak to the sky and convince the clouds to rain on their land, but nothing good came out of it.

One day when Modjadji was staring at the empty
water pot on top of the hill she noticed that a great
cloud, all dark and heavy with rain, was slowly
approaching her village. The grass on the ground
was all brown and dead. It needed the rain from
the cloud overhead. The cows mooed for the rain
to fall from the sky and people looked up and then
to their empty wells and water pots.

But the big black cloud, all heavy with rain, was now very slowly moving away from Modjadji's village. Modjadji felt that she needed to do something. The cloud looked like a big balloon full of water. If only somehow, she could pop it, but how? Then she noticed an eagle which was circling above her head. Modjadji recognised the eagle. It was Thunder! The eagle dropped a beautiful feather that fell at Modjadji's feet.

She picked it up and put it together with a slender stick. With all her might Modjadji shot the arrow into the sky. It pierced the cloud and released the rain with a very loud noise. Rain began to fall, and it did not stop for three days.

People started dancing, cows started mooing with happiness and slowly the grass turned green again. The people of that land called Modjadji 'The Rain Queen'. They believe her to have special powers, including the ability to control the clouds and rainfall.

Everyone wanted Modjadji to take over after her father and retain the title of the Rain Queen. From that day to this day, in certain parts of southern Africa, there has always been a rain queen.

Pankaj Sulodia is a Steiner-Waldorf teacher, currently teaching at Ringwood Waldorf School.

Octavia Spinney, now a pupil in the upper school at Ringwood Waldorf School, is a creative and budding artist. Octavia thoroughly enjoyed making illustrations for this book and is looking forward to establishing herself within the art community.

Ringwood Waldorf School, Folly Farm Lane, Ashley, Ringwood
Hampshire, BH24 2NN

Printed in Great Britain
by Amazon